Kapaemahu

by **Hinaleimoana Wong-Kalu,**
Dean Hamer, *and* **Joe Wilson**

Illustrated by **Daniel Sousa**

Kokila

Kokila

An imprint of Penguin Random House LLC, New York

First published in the United States of America
by Kokila, an imprint of Penguin Random House LLC, 2022

Kokila & colophon are registered trademarks of Penguin Random House LLC.
Visit us online at penguinrandomhouse.com.

Library of Congress Cataloging-in-Publication Data is available.

Manufactured in China

ISBN 9780593530061

1 3 5 7 9 10 8 6 4 2
TOPL

Design by Jasmin Rubero
Text set in Plantin MT Pro

For KT—Koe ta koe o hoku mafu. My mirror and twin flame,
my inspiration and hero. Forever is a place . . . and I will see you there.
And for Kauai Iki, my mentor, friend, and sister. Mahalo for shining the
light on the road to freedom. Be true to myself I shall.
—H. W. K.

For all those whose history has been ignored and erased.
This is your time.
—D. H. and J. W.

For Liz and Alina.
—D. S.

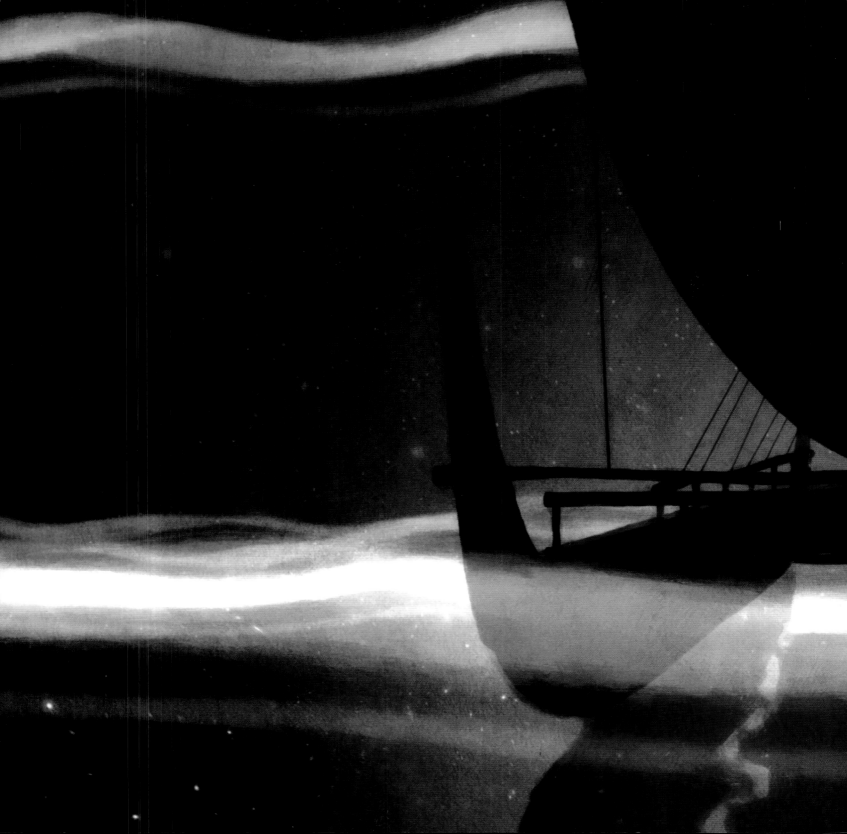

I te au ma mua o to Kakukihewa noho
alii ia Oahu, aia no he eha mau kanaka
tupaianaha o ta holo moana a haele mai
lakou mai Moaulanuiakea a tu mai i
Hawaii nei.

Long ago, before Kakuhihewa ruled Oahu,
four Tahitians journeyed across the ocean
from their home in Moaulanuiakea to Hawaii.

A pae akula a noho i Ulukou ma Waikiki.

They settled at Ulukou in Waikiki.

A oia mau malihini he ui kanaka leo maliu, a he nonohe waipahe no nae.

The visitors were tall and deep in voice yet gentle and soft-spoken.

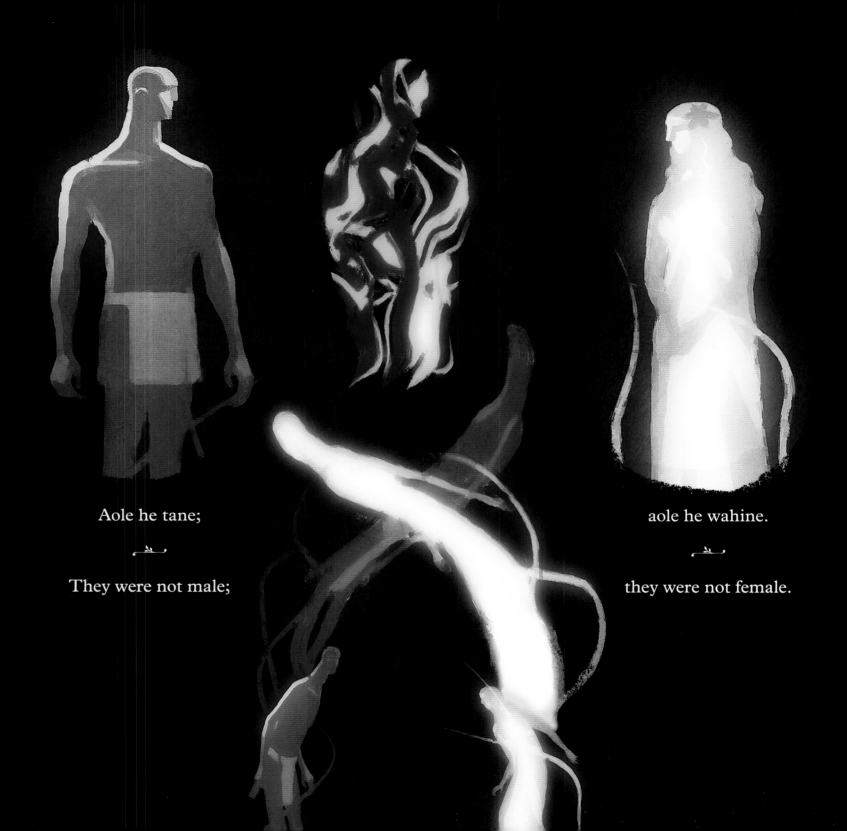

Aole he tane;

aole he wahine.

They were not male;

they were not female.

He mau mahu lakou—
He palua nohoi lakou ma ka naau me ka noonoo
a ma na ano apau.

They were mahu—
a mixture of both in mind, heart, and spirit.

A o ta inoa o ta lakou alakai oia no
o Kapaemahu. He mau hiwahiwa
a na atua o ia mau tahuna lapaau.

O Kapuni, mana nui.

Indeed, the leader of the group
was named Kapae*mahu*. The Gods
favored the four visitors with skill
in the science of healing.

Kapuni possessed great spiritual
power.

O Kinohi, wanana ite papalua.

Kinohi was all-seeing.

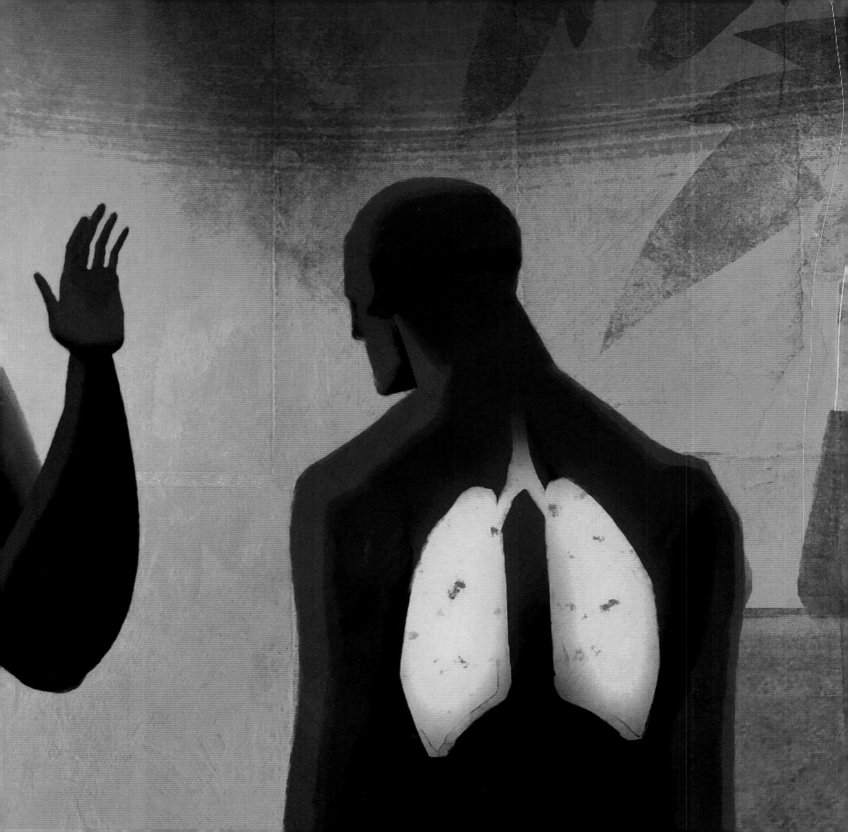

O Kahaloa, me tana laau tahea.

Kahaloa could heal from afar.

A o Kapaemahu, o ka tau laau.

And Kapaemahu healed by laying on hands.

Ua kaana mai no lakou i to lakou ite me to lakou naauao
i na kanaka o ia pae aina.

⟩⟩

They bequeathed their healing wisdom to the people
of these islands.

A lawa pono ta lakou hana, a makatau e haalele, hu ka iini e mahalo i ia poe tahuna lapaau me ka tutulu aku i kahi mea hoomanao ia lakou.

When the healers had completed their work, the people wished to express their gratitude for their wondrous cures by erecting a monument in their honor.

I ta po tane lakou i naue ai a ua atoatoa lakou ma Kaimuki,
he wahi taulana i ta pohatu kani.

One moonless night, they gathered at Kaimuki, an area
famous for its bell rock.

Naue aku me eha mau pohatu nunui a hiti loa i Waikiki.

They moved four great boulders all the way to Waikiki.

A ulu mai ka la, waiho akula lakou i ta lakou mana lapaau me ta kanu pu ketahi i mau tii hoomana ma lalo o ta pohatu taitahi.

As the sun rose, the healers began to transfer their powers into the stones, placing idols representing the dual spirit of mahu under each one.

A hala no hootahi mahina.
O ta haalele no ia o Kapaemahu ma aohe loa e hoi hou mai.

The ceremonies lasted a full moon.
Then, knowing that their healing powers were safe in the stones,
the mahu vanished.

He mau sehetuha i moe ai ia mau pohatu ma kahatai.

The stones remained a sacred site for centuries.

A hala te au,
a loli loa no.

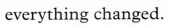

But as the tides of time passed,
everything changed.

A nalo wale ia moaukala no Kapaemahu, nalohia me ua mau pohatu ma lalo o kahi tahua hale kinipopo olokaa.

⌁

The stones of Kapaemahu were forgotten, even buried under a bowling alley.

Oiai no, ua wehe hou ia mai ia mau pohatu eha. Pela no o ta
kulana mahu oia mau tahuna lapaau i hoonalo ia ma ta ha
moolelo mai no Kapaemahu.

⚬

The stones have since been recovered. But their history is still
being suppressed, and the fact that the healers were mahu has
been erased.

Auwe ka minamina nohoi. Aloha.
Te oe maopopo i ta moaukala o ia mau pohatu,
alaila oe ike i to lakou mana ola.

It's a great loss. A deep shame.
For only when you understand the true history of
these stones shall you behold their living power.

Te no katou e taana aku a e tutala aku i na moolelo
o to katou poe tupuna o te au i hala, pela no katou
e mahalo a e hoohanohano aku ai ia lakou a me ta
lakou hooilina o ka naauao.

Ola ola ola,
e ola loa ta moolelo no Kapaemahu.

And when you share that story, you honor it.

Life, life, life . . .
Long life to the story of Kapaemahu.

AUTHORS' NOTES

I am Kanaka—a native person descended from the original inhabitants of the islands of Hawaii. Our survival as Indigenous people depends on our ability to know and practice our cultural traditions, to speak and understand our language, and to feel an authentic connection to our own history.

It is our duty as native people to render our narratives from the heartset and mindset of our ancestors and how they saw the world. That is why I wanted to write a bilingual film and book about Kapaemahu using Olelo Niihau—the only form of Hawaiian that has been continuously spoken since prior to the arrival of foreigners. It is not enough to study our language in an American classroom nor to read about our history in an English-language textbook. We need to be active participants in telling our own stories in our own way.

I am also mahu, which, like many Indigenous third-gender identities, was once respected but is now more often a target for hatred and discrimination. I want our young people to understand that the ability to embrace both the male and female aspects of their spirit is not a weakness but a strength, a reason to rejoice and not fear.

I am grateful to everyone who helped me learn and grow within my culture: my grandparents, parents, and other family members, kumu and kupuna, and my extended Niihau family who empowered me through our language. I am also appreciative for those who care for the stones today, and trust that readers of this book who have an opportunity to visit Waikiki will respect them as well, bringing only their words and prayers to honor this sacred site.

—Hinaleimoana Wong-Kalu

We rolled out the film on which this book is based during the worst public health crisis in modern history. Perhaps Hawaiians' holistic approach to well-being can help begin the healing that is so needed for the many different consequences of the pandemic. This has also been a time of great debate over the meaning of monuments, and we hope *Kapaemahu* will broaden the discussion by focusing on a site that honors true heroes from the past.

As partners in life and filmmaking for more than twenty years, we are especially excited about bringing this story to the next generation, who often have an easier time than their parents in accepting that not everybody is the same. We first heard about the stones of Kapaemahu from Hina, who we were filming for a documentary about her work as a teacher, and we are honored and delighted to be continuing our collaboration on our fifth project together. We are also especially grateful to Pacific Islanders in Communications for its unwavering support.

—Dean Hamer and Joe Wilson

HISTORY OF THE HEALER STONES

This book is based on the moolelo of *The Healer Stones of Kapaemahu*—a traditional Hawaiian story that took place many centuries ago. Originally the story was passed on orally from one generation to the next, but fortunately it was recorded in writing at the turn of the twentieth century. The conveyor was James Aalapuna Harbottle Boyd, a notable Hawaiian who was fluent in both Hawaiian and English and a confidante of the royal family. The handwritten manuscript of his story became the basis for the script of our animated film *Kapaemahu* and the text of this book.

The monumental stones described in the story remained a sacred spot on Waikiki Beach from the ancient past through the time of Princess Likelike and her daughter Kaiulani, the last heir apparent to the throne of the Hawaiian Kingdom, who prayed and placed seaweed lei on them before swimming in the ocean nearby. Recognizing the importance of the site, Princess Likelike's husband, Governor Archibald Cleghorn, had the stones excavated and grouped together for safekeeping on their beachfront property in front of the royal estate of Ainahau. But colonization, militarization, and the growth of tourism led to deep changes in all aspects of Hawaiian life and culture, and in 1941 the stones were buried to make room for a bowling alley in rapidly developing Waikiki.

When the bowling alley was demolished in 1963, a few elders, including revered Hawaiian scholar Mary Kawena Pukui, remembered the sacred stones and insisted they be recovered. Following another move to make way for a public restroom, the stones were installed in their current location on the beach, on top of a raised platform behind an iron fence.

Despite the physical protection afforded to the stones, the history behind them was suppressed to conceal the fact that the healers were mahu—extraordinary individuals of both male and female spirit—and that their spiritual duality was intrinsic to their healing power. This censoring coincided with a period of great prejudice and discrimination against gender minorities, including an anti-cross-dressing law in Hawaii that necessitated mahu showgirls to wear an "I Am a Boy" button to avoid arrest.

Today, the stones are located on one of the busiest stretches of Waikiki Beach, but few of the millions of passersby know their true story. We hope this book will help restore the stones as a monument to the extraordinary skills, talents, and accomplishments of the Kapaemahu healers. They are heroes, and their stones provide a permanent reminder of Hawaii's long history of healing and inclusion.

OLELO NIIHAU

This book is written in Olelo Niihau, which is the form of Hawaiian spoken by the fewer than 100 Native Hawaiian residents of the island of Niihau, westernmost of the 8 main Hawaiian islands, and by descendants of Niihau ancestry living on the adjacent western end of the island of Kauai. We chose to use the Niihau dialect because it is the only uninterrupted form of Hawaiian in continuous communal use since prior to the arrival of foreigners, and it is also closest to the Southern Polynesian dialects that might have been spoken by the healers. We articulated the story as it would have been spoken in colloquial Niihau form and wrote the text in this style, omitting all diacritical markings as well. Our aim was to present the story in as close as possible to its original form and perspective.

The Healer Stones of Kapaemahu, like all moolelo, is a mix of history and legend with multiple versions. While our book is based on the earliest recorded version, there may be others yet to be told.

GLOSSARY

Aloha: Greetings—hello, goodbye, love, affection, respect, expression of great regret.

Lapaau: Medicinal healing.

Mahu: An individual with a blend of male and female mind, heart, and spirit.

Mana: Spiritual power, strength, energy, ability.

Moolelo: Story, history, narrative.

Ola: Life, health.

Pohaku: Stone, rock, boulder.